Baby Pig

By P. Mignon Hinds
Illustrated by Jim Kritz

A GOLDEN BOOK • NEW YORK
Western Publishing Company, Inc., Racine, Wisconsin 53404

The sun's rays peek through the darkness. A rooster calls out "cock-a-doodle-doo!" All the little pigs are sound asleep in their warm, straw bed. But Baby Pig is wide awake.

Baby Pig jostles her brothers and sisters. They squeal
noisily until each one finds a place to nurse along
Mother Pig's warm belly. Baby Pig has waited too
long. There is no room for her. That does not stop
Baby Pig. She just squeezes in between two of her
brothers.

When Baby Pig has had her fill, she gets up on her short legs and runs out of the shed. More piglets come to join Baby Pig's running game. They chase and bump each other. Baby Pig gets a surprise thump from her brother.

Suddenly, Baby Pig comes face to face with the barnyard rooster. The rooster looks at her with his small, darting eyes. But Baby Pig does not like to be stared at.

Baby Pig's loud squeals bring Mother Pig hurrying to protect her young one. The huge sow barks to warn the rooster that he is not welcome.

Too much bright sunlight makes Baby Pig feel hot and uncomfortable. She finds a large patch of mud and lies down for a nice long wallow. Baby Pig rolls around in the cool, dark mud until she is almost completely covered.

After her mudbath, Baby Pig rubs against a fencepost. This is how she gets rid of any insects that might have been caught on her short, bristly coat.

Just then, the farmer comes with a load of grain. He wants the six-week-old pigs to begin eating grown-up pig food. Soon Baby Pig and her brothers and sisters won't drink their mother's milk at all.

Nice and full, Baby Pig sniffs the ground. Suddenly, she sees something move! It is a grasshopper. Baby Pig tries to get closer, but the insect jumps away before Baby Pig can catch it.

Mother Pig rounds up her babies. She leads them up
the ramp and into the shed. Baby Pig takes one last
look around, then runs and catches up with her
brothers and sisters.

When evening comes, Baby Pig still wants
to play, but her brothers and sisters are tired.

Finally, she settles down beside her
mother and falls fast asleep.

Facts About Baby Pig (A Chesterwhite Pig)

Where Do Pigs Live?

Pigs live on farms throughout the United States. Many pig farms are in midwest states, including Iowa, Illinois, Indiana and Missouri. Minnesota, Nebraska, Ohio and South Dakota are other states in America's corn belt where large numbers of pigs are raised. Farmers build pens or barns with warm, comfortable straw floors as pig homes. During the day, pigs often stay outside in the farm pasture.

What Do Pigs Eat?

When pigs are old enough, they can eat just about anything! But farmers make sure that their pigs eat a healthy diet of grains, protein, vitamins and minerals. Baby piglets usually nurse on their mothers' milk for three to six weeks. Then they are fed corn, sorghum, barley, wheat, rye and oat grains. They also help themselves to soybean and linseed oils, meat scraps and other animal parts. Pigs need salt as well as pasture crops like alfalfa and clover. In spite of what many people think, these animals know when they have eaten enough. They do not eat too much.

How Do Pigs Communicate?

Pigs have their own language. Happy pigs grunt to show satisfaction. Hungry pigs roar. Baby piglets will squeal when they are afraid or excited. A bark or woof is an alarm or warning.

How Big Are Pigs and How Long Do They Live?

Baby Chester White pigs weigh about two and a half pounds at birth. They grow very fast, and might gain one and one-half pounds each day. Pigs become full grown when they are close to two years old. Adult female sows and male boars can weigh nearly one thousand pounds, but they average between six hundred to eight hundred pounds. Most hogs only live on farms until they are about six months old and have grown to around two hundred pounds.

What Is A Pig's Family Like?

Mother sows usually have eight to twelve babies at a time. A few days before piglets are born, many farmers wash the mother and put her in a clean pen. Some farms have a separate stall or small space for each mother. In cold weather, farmers may put a heat lamp in the pen to keep baby piglets warm. Most sows give birth to two litters each year.

What Are Pigs Raised For?

Pigs are raised mainly for their meat. They provide the bacon, ham, pork and sausage that people eat. The fat, hair and skin of these important farm animals are also used to make lard, brushes, leather, soap, glue and other products.